My Weirder-est School #4

Miss Blake Is a Flake!

Dan Gutman

Pictures by Jim Paillot

HARPER
An Imprint of HarperCollinsPublishers

To Daniel Christie

My Weirder-est School #4: Miss Blake Is a Flake!

www.harpercollinschildrens.com

ISBN 978-0-06-269110-1 (pbk. bdg.) – ISBN 978-0-06-269111-8 (library bdg.)

Typography by Laura Mock
20 21 22 23 24 PC/BRR 10 9 8 7 6 5 4 3 2 1
❖
First Edition

Contents

Math

A.J.
RYAN
MICHAEL
EXIA
ANDREA
EMILY
NEIL

Cheese Doesn't Have Ears

My name is A.J. and I hate getting my picture taken.

Why do we always have to say "cheese" when somebody takes our picture? What does cheese have to do with anything?

I guess it might make sense if you were taking a picture of a piece of cheese.

But why would anybody take a picture of cheese? And even if you were crazy enough to take pictures of cheese, why would you bother *saying* "cheese" out loud? The cheese can't hear you. Cheese doesn't have ears.

Anyway, the guys and I had just finished lunch in the vomitorium, and we scraped off our plates. Our plan was to go out on the monkey bars during recess and play with our Striker Smith action figures. Striker Smith is a superhero from the future who fights crime. As I was taking Striker out of my backpack, I noticed a flyer taped to a table. It said . . .

We all got excited. It said there was going to be a meeting in the vomitorium on Friday night.

"I always wanted to be a Beaver Scout," said Neil, who we call the nude kid even though he wears clothes.

Beaver Scouts are cool. My friend Billy who lives around the corner is a Beaver Scout. He gets to wear a uniform and win cool badges and stuff. Billy's always going on camping trips, and he told me Beaver Scouts get to do cool stuff like shoot bows and arrows, make rockets, and blow stuff up.

I'm not sure Beaver Scouts really get to blow stuff up. But I do know that they get to make campfires. Burning stuff up is almost as cool as blowing stuff up.

And the best part about being a Beaver Scout—no girls are allowed!

"I'm joining up," I said.

"Me too," said Michael, who never ties his shoes.

"Me three," said Ryan, who will eat anything, even stuff that isn't food.

But you'll never believe who walked by the table at that moment. It was two girls from our class, annoying Andrea and crybaby Emily.

"Shhhhh!" Ryan whispered as the girls approached. "Don't tell Andrea and Emily we're going to be Beaver Scouts! They'll be jealous."

I sat on the edge of the table so Andrea and Emily wouldn't see the Beaver Scout announcement.

We all started whistling to let the girls know we weren't hiding something. Because when you're whistling, you can't be hiding anything.*

"Whatcha doing, Arlo?" asked Andrea, who calls me by my real name because she knows I don't like it.

"Nothing," I said. "Hanging out. We're

* It's impossible to whistle and hide something at the same time. Nobody knows why.

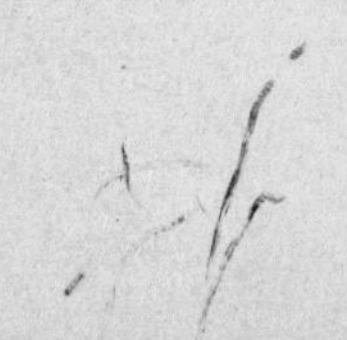

not hiding anything."

"Why are you sitting on the table?" Emily asked. "It's recess. We get to go outside."

"None of your beeswax," I replied. "We're just playing with Striker Smith."

"Fine," Andrea said as she scraped her tray into the garbage can. "Have fun playing with your doll, Arlo."

"It's not a *doll*!" I shouted at her. "It's an action figure!"

"Call it what you want," Andrea said, rolling her eyes. "Come on, Emily. Let's play in the playground."

2

Say Cheese!

We had to wait a million hundred days for the Beaver Scout meeting. But it was okay, because the flyer said we needed to wear the official Beaver Scout uniform. So my parents and I went on the official Beaver Scout website to buy an official Beaver Scout uniform.

On the website, they sell all kinds of stuff Beaver Scouts need–official Beaver Scout sleeping bags, official Beaver Scout tents, official Beaver Scout bug spray, and even official Beaver Scout toiletries.*

Finally, we found the page with the uniform. It's cool. It's brown, with a Beaver Scout patches and stripes on the sleeves. It comes with a cap that has a *B* on it and an official Beaver Scout neckerchief. A neckerchief is a lot like a handkerchief, except you wear it around your neck and you don't blow your nose into it.

My parents ordered all that stuff. It cost them a million dollars. Plus shipping. I

---

* Wow, I didn't know that toilets grow on trees.

guess that means a ship delivers the stuff to your house. No wonder it costs so much money.

We were afraid the Beaver Scout uniform wouldn't arrive in time for the first meeting. But that morning, we got a package in the mail. The regular mailman brought it. There was no ship.

I ran upstairs to try on my uniform. It looked cool. I came downstairs and made a grand entrance for my parents and my sister, Amy.

"You look *soooo* handsome, A.J.," my mom said. She was getting a little choked up as she took pictures of me in my Beaver Scout uniform.

"What a dweeb," commented my sister.

We drove to school. When I got out of the car, I saw Ryan, Michael, and Neil in their Beaver Scout uniforms.

Ryan's mom is really emotional, and she was wiping tears from her eyes. "You boys are getting so big," she blubbered. "Look at my baby Ryan. It seems like only yesterday that you were in diapers."

"You were wearing diapers yesterday?" I asked Ryan.

"We need to take pictures!" my mother said, pulling out her cell phone.

"Yes!" agreed all the parents.

Ugh. Parents *love* taking pictures.

"Do we *have* to?" I asked.

“Of *course* we have to,” my mother said. “This is a milestone.”

With grown-ups, *everything* is a milestone. You could burp and my mother would act like you graduated from college. When grown-ups want to take pictures, there's no stopping them.

"Say cheese!" my mom ordered, pointing her phone at me.

"Cheese," I grumbled.

After that, she took a picture of my dad and me together. Then she took a picture of me and my sister. Then she took a picture of me and my dad and my sister. Then she took a picture of my dad and my sister. Then she asked my dad to take a picture of me and her. Then she asked me to take a picture of her and Dad. Then she asked me to take a picture of her and my sister. Then she asked Ryan's dad to take a picture of our whole family.

I thought I was gonna die of old age. When grown-ups take a picture, they have to get a shot of every possible combination of people. That's the first rule of being a grown-up.

Finally, we finished the picture-taking and went into the vomitorium.

"I wonder who your Beaver Scout leader will be," my dad said.

And you'll never believe who walked through the door at that moment.

Nobody! You can't walk through a door! Doors are made of wood. But you'll never believe who walked through the door*way*.

You probably think it was the Beaver

Scout leader. But it wasn't. So nah-nah-nah boo-boo on you.

It was Andrea, Emily, and Alexia! And they were wearing Beaver Scout uniforms!

It's a Tough World Out There

"*Eeeeeeeek!*" I screamed. "Girls! Who let *you* in here? Girls can't be Beaver Scouts!"

"They can too!" Andrea replied.

"Can not!" I said.

We went back and forth like that for a while.

"They changed the rules, Arlo," Andrea said. "Boys *and* girls can be Beaver Scouts.

This is the twenty-first century, you know."

I knew perfectly well what century it was. What did that have to do with anything?

I was going to say something mean to Andrea, but I didn't have the chance. Because you'll never believe who poked her head into the door at that moment.

Nobody! Poking your head into a door would hurt. I thought we went over that in Chapter 2. But you'll never believe who poked her head into the door*way*.

"A ten . . . shun!" a lady shouted.

I had no idea what that meant, but everybody else did, because they all stood up straight, the way soldiers do in the army.

"I'm Miss Blake," the lady barked. "I'm your Beaver Scout leader."

Miss Blake was wearing a Beaver Scout uniform like mine, but with a cooler shoulder patch. She looked mean.

"Hello, Miss Blake," my dad said, sticking out his hand to shake. "We're so happy to–"

But my dad didn't have the chance to finish his sentence.

"All parents out of the room!" barked Miss Blake.

"Can we just stand in the back and take a few pictures?" my mom asked.

"No!" barked Miss Blake.* "Parents, get *out*!"

The parents made a beeline for the door. That was weird, because I've never seen bees get in a line. They usually just fly around every which way.

"Are we going to learn how to blow stuff up?" I asked after all the parents were gone.

"No!" barked Miss Blake. "Line up for inspection, in size order!"

We all pringled up. I had to stand in front of Andrea, who's the tallest kid in our class. Emily is the shortest. She looked like she was going to cry, as usual.

---

* She sure barks a lot. I thought only dogs bark. Well, dogs and trees.

Miss Blake walked down the line, looking everybody over.

"Disgraceful!" she barked at Emily. "Stop whimpering like a jellyfish!"

"Filthy!" she barked at Michael. "Tie your shoes!"

"Disgusting!" she barked at Neil. "Comb your hair!"

"Slovenly!" she barked at Ryan. "Trim your fingernails!"

"A mess!" she barked at Alexia. "Neatness counts!"

Miss Blake was standing in front of me. She looked me up and down. I was shaking with fear. I thought I was gonna die. She stuck her face about two inches from mine.

"I heard what you said when I came into the room, buster," she barked at me. "Do you have a problem with girls?"

"Uh, no, sir," I said. "I mean Miss . . . I mean ma'am . . . I mean–" I didn't know what to call her.

"You'd better not!" Miss Blake barked in my face. "Your mother was a girl once, you know."

"Just once?" I asked. "I thought she was a girl *all* the time."

Everybody giggled even though I hadn't said anything funny.

"Are you trying to be smart, buster?" Miss Blake sneered at me.

I wasn't sure how to answer that. Don't we go to school to be smart? Isn't being smart a good thing? "Yes" seemed to be the answer. But from the look on her face, she *didn't* want me to say I was trying to be smart. And if I said I *wasn't* trying to be smart, that would mean I was trying to be dumb. I didn't know what to say.

"I've got my eye on *you*, buster," Miss Blake said.

What did I do? And why was she calling me buster?

Miss Blake moved on to Andrea, looking her up and down.

"Very nice," she said. "This girl is neat, her hair is in place, her fingernails are trimmed, her posture is good, and she looks confident. I'm going to give you a sticker."

The sticker said BEST LINER UPPER on it.

What?! That's not fair! Nobody lines up better than me.

Actually, I didn't care, because stickers are lame. Grown-ups always think they're doing us a big favor by giving us stickers.

They're just pieces of paper with sticky stuff on the back. If you want to give me something, give me a video game.

But Andrea acted like Miss Blake had just given her a million dollars.

"Thank you, Miss Blake!" Andrea said. Then she smiled the smile that she smiles to let everybody know she got something that nobody else got. Why can't a truck full of stickers fall on Andrea's head?

Miss Blake wheeled around to face the group.

"The rest of you are *pathetic*!" she barked. "But I'll whip you kids into shape. By the time I'm done, you'll be spitting nails."

That sounded kind of cool, actually.

"Excuse me," said Alexia, raising her hand. "I thought we were going to sell cookies, and do arts and crafts projects."

"Cookies?" snorted Miss Blake. "Arts and crafts? That stuff is for wimps. It's a tough world out there, and the sooner you get tough, the better. Did I tell you about the time I was attacked by a bear?"

"Uh, we just met like a minute ago," I said quietly.

"I was on a fifty-mile hike," said Miss Blake, "and I suddenly noticed a bear was stalking me. He was getting closer and closer."

"What did you do?" asked Andrea.

"I punched his face in!" barked Miss Blake. "*That's* what I did! It was a matter of survival!"

The thought of Miss Blake punching a bear was funny to me. I peeked at Ryan. He was peeking at me. He made a funny face, and I started giggling. I couldn't help it. Miss Blake wheeled around and glared at me.

"You think this is *funny*, buster?" she barked. "You think I'm *joking*? Well, since you like jokes so much, I'll tell you a joke. Why did the chicken cross the road?"

"Uh, to get to the other side?"

"No!" barked Miss Blake. "That brave chicken crossed the road to save his

injured buddy, who had just been run over by a train. It was lying there, dying. That chicken risked his life to save his friend. Never leave your buddy behind. That's *my* kind of joke."

It didn't seem like a very funny joke to me.

Miss Blake is a flake.

“I call this meeting of the Beaver Scouts to order,” barked Miss Blake. “We begin and end each meeting with the Beaver Growl.”

What? Cows moo. Ducks quack. Pigs oink. Beavers . . .

“What sound does a beaver make?” Ryan whispered.

"Beats me," I whispered back. "I didn't even know they made sounds."

Miss Blake got down on her hands and knees and started to scurry around on the floor, making weird noises.

"Get on the ground!" she barked. "Growl like a busy beaver!"

We all got down on the floor and growled.

"Okay," Miss Blake said as she jumped up. "It's time for the official Beaver Scout promise. It's very simple. Three little words."

Miss Blake held up her right hand,

closed her eyes, and announced, "Do your duty."

We all giggled because Miss Blake said "duty," which sounds just like "doody." It's okay to say "duty," but we're not allowed to say "doody." Nobody knows why. They should really have two different-sounding words for those things. It would make life a lot easier.

Next, Miss Blake handed each of us the Beaver Scout Handbook.*

"I want you to take this home and memorize it word for word," she barked. "This book could save your life one day."

---

* Why do they call it a handbook? What else are you going to hold the book with? Your feet?

Books? Ugh. Books are boring. I don't even know why you're reading this one.

I leafed through the handbook. It had lots of activities in it—making campfires, tying knots, studying insects, learning about astronomy, tracking weather, boating and canoeing, spelunking . . .

Spelunking?

"What's spelunking?" I asked.

"Spelunking is exploring caves," said Little Miss I-Know-Everything.

That's a weird word. Why don't they just call it exploring caves? Why did they need to invent some dumb word that nobody knows?

"As you master activities in your

handbook, you earn awards," barked Miss Blake. "First you get a sticker just for trying a new activity."

"I love stickers!" shouted Andrea.

"Then, as you get better, you'll earn a decal," said Miss Blake, showing us a page in the handbook that had pictures of decals.

"Decals are cool!" said Emily.

"After that, you'll earn a ribbon," said Miss Blake.

"I like ribbons!" said Alexia.

"Then you can earn a badge," said Miss Blake.

"I've always wanted a badge!" said Ryan.

"Then you'll earn a belt loop," said Miss Blake.

Belt loops are metal loops that you put on your belt, so they have the perfect name.

"Then you'll earn a certificate," said Miss Blake.

"I can put that on my wall!" said Neil.

"Then you'll earn a medallion," said Miss Blake.

"I can hang that around my neck!" said Michael.

"Then you'll earn a plaque," said Miss Blake.

"I have that on my teeth!" I said.

"Not *that* kind of plaque, dumbhead!" said Andrea.

"Oh snap!" said Ryan.

All that stuff sounded like a bunch of

junk to me. I'd rather win nothing, stay home, and play video games.

"Finally," said Miss Blake, "I will award the trophy for the Busy Beaver of the Year." She showed us a picture of a big trophy.

"Ooooh," we all oohed.

The whole time, Andrea was taking notes in a notebook. She carries a notebook *everywhere.* Andrea loves winning stuff. She doesn't even care what it is.

"Okay," said Miss Blake, "it's time for us to sing the Beaver Scout song. Turn to page twenty-three in your handbook."

"I love singing!" said Andrea.

"The official Beaver Scout song is 'Whip Whap Willie,'" said Miss Blake. "*Whip whap* is the sound of a beaver tail hitting the water. We sing it to the tune of 'Old MacDonald.' Ready? Sing!"

We all started singing . . .

Whip Whap Willie had a tail,
E-I-E-I-O.
And with that tail he whacked a snail,
E-I-E-I-O.
With a whip whip here,
And a whap whap there,
Here a whip,
There a whap,
Everywhere a whip whap.
Whip Whap Willie had a tail,
E-I-E-I-O!

That had to be the lamest song in the history of the world. But Andrea was belting it out like she was on Broadway. What is her problem?

"Okay, that concludes this meeting of the Beaver Scouts," said Miss Blake.

"Are we going to go spelunking?" Neil asked.

"No!" barked Miss Blake.

"When do we get to blow stuff up?" I asked.

"Never!"

"So . . . we can go home?" Michael asked.

"No!" barked Miss Blake. "First we have to do the Beaver Growl."

We got down on all fours again and

scurried around the floor, making beaver sounds.

I wonder if *real* beavers get together each week and act like people. They would probably stand up on their hind legs and chat about the weather or sing songs about what they were going to eat for dinner.

That would be weird.

The next meeting of the Beaver Scouts was in the gym at school. Miss Blake was waiting for us.

"I hope you all memorized the Beaver Scout Handbook," she barked.

"I did!" shouted Andrea, who always does anything grown-ups tell her to do.

"Can I get a drink of water?" asked Neil.

"No!" barked Miss Blake. "Water is for wimps. What if you're out in the desert and there's no water? Today we're going to learn survival skills."

"I thought Beaver scouting was gonna be *fun*," I grumbled under my breath.

"It's not about *fun*, buster!" barked Miss Blake. "Beaver scouting is about survival! It's dog-eat-dog out there."

I didn't know that dogs eat other dogs. But what did dog food have to do with anything?

"Let's warm up with some jumping jacks!" barked Miss Blake.

Ugh. I hate jumping jacks. Who came

up with *that* idea?*

"Jumping jacks are fun!" shouted Andrea.

"ONE . . . TWO . . . THREE . . . FOUR . . ."

We did about a million hundred jumping jacks. I thought I was gonna die. By the end, Andrea was the only one who was still jumping, so Miss Blake gave her a decal. Not fair!

"On to the obstacle course!" barked Miss Blake. She had set up a long line of upside-down desks, buckets, brooms, barrels, and all kinds of other junk. We had to crawl under, around, and over all that

---

* It was probably some guy named Jack who had too much time on his hands.

stuff to get to the other side of the gym.

"This is going to prepare you for the real world," barked Miss Blake. "Go! Go! Go!"

One by one, we ran the obstacle course. I thought I was gonna throw up.

"I don't see how this prepares us for the real world," I grumbled.

"Enemy planes are dropping bombs on you!" barked Miss Blake. "Get down low!"

She used a stopwatch to see how long it took each of us to get through the obstacle course. Naturally, Andrea had the fastest time, so Miss Blake gave her a ribbon. Not fair!

"Next, it's time to jump over chairs!" barked Miss Blake.

"Jumping over chairs is fun!" shouted Andrea.

"Why would we ever have to jump over chairs in the real world?" complained Ryan.

"What if you're in a jungle and you get attacked by alligators?" asked Miss Blake. "You'll need to jump over them to escape."

"I would just punch their faces in," I said.

"That's inappropriate, Arlo," said Andrea. "I don't approve of violence."

"What do you have against violins?" I asked.

"Not violins! Violence!"

I was just yanking Andrea's chain. But Little Miss Perfect could jump over more chairs than anybody, of course. So Miss Blake gave her a badge. Not fair!

"Let's move on to the climbing wall!" barked Miss Blake.

One wall of the gym had little knobs all over it so we could grab on with our hands and push up with our feet. It was still really hard to climb.

"Climbing a wall is fun!" shouted Andrea.

Needless to say, she was able to climb the wall faster than anybody else. Miss Blake gave Andrea a belt loop. Not fair!

"Next, it's time to climb the rope!" barked Miss Blake.

There was a thick rope hanging from the ceiling of the gym.

"Climbing rope is fun!" shouted Andrea,

who immediately started climbing as if she had been doing it all her life.

"Why do we have to climb a rope?" asked Michael. "When are we ever going to have to do that?"

"What if you're in the forest and a bear attacks you?" asked Miss Blake. "You see a vine nearby. You climb it. You save your life. *That's* why we climb the rope."

Miss Blake must have a thing about bears.

"Why can't we just punch the bear's face in?" I suggested.

I don't have to tell you which one of us was the best at climbing the rope. Miss Blake gave Andrea a certificate. Not fair!

In the far corner of the gym was a big barbell. It looked like it weighed a million hundred pounds.

"Okay, let's see who can pick up this weight!" barked Miss Blake.

"Why?" asked Alexia. "I'm not going to be a weight lifter when I grow up."

"What if you're in the wilderness and a boulder falls on your head?" asked Miss Blake. "What are you going to do?"

"Punch the boulder's face in?" I suggested.

I tried to pick up the barbell, but it was way too heavy.

Ryan tried to pick up the barbell. He couldn't.

Michael tried to pick it up. He couldn't.

We *all* tried to pick up the barbell. Even Andrea couldn't pick it up.

"It's impossible," said Emily.

"Of course it's impossible!" barked Miss Blake. "You've got to work *together*! Teamwork makes the dream work!"

We all grabbed the barbell at the same time. We picked it up!

"Good work!" barked Miss Blake. "Now it's time for your final survival challenge. This is where we separate the men from the boys."

Huh? There weren't any men around. I

didn't know what she was talking about.

Miss Blake led us over to a long table with chairs around it. She pulled out a bag of marshmallows.

"I call this 'The Marshmallow Challenge,'" she said.

All right! At last there was a challenge I could win. Nobody can eat more marshmallows than me. I *love* marshmallows.

Miss Blake told us to sit at the table. Then she put a marshmallow in front of each of us.

"Here's the challenge," she said. "I'll give you that marshmallow right now if you want. Or, if you wait fifteen minutes, you can eat *two* marshmallows."

"HUH?" we all said, which is also HUH backward.

"So if we eat our marshmallow now, we won't get another one?" asked Alexia.

"That's right," said Miss Blake. "But if you wait fifteen minutes, you'll get a second marshmallow. Starting . . . *now*!" She clicked her stopwatch.

I looked at my marshmallow.

"I'm going to wait," Andrea said. "I'd rather have two marshmallows in fifteen minutes than one marshmallow now."

"Me too," said Emily, who always does everything Andrea does.

Hmmm. Waiting for stuff is *hard*. When I want something, I want it *now*. And I could eat marshmallows for breakfast, lunch, and dinner.

The marshmallow looked so good. I could almost taste the creamy sweetness. It was just sitting on the table in front of me, waiting to be eaten.

I reached my hand out toward my marshmallow. Maybe I could just take a little bite of it to tide me over for fifteen minutes.

"No taking little bites of your marsh-mallow!" barked Miss Blake.

"Just wait, A.J.," said Ryan. "Then you get twice as many marshmallows. Fifteen minutes isn't so long."

Fifteen minutes is a *long* time. It's almost an hour.

I gave up. I picked up my marshmallow and popped it into my mouth. Yum!

"Ha! I knew you'd give in, Arlo!" shouted Andrea. "Anything you can do, I can do better. I can do anything better than you."

"No you can't," I replied.

"Yes I can," she said.

"No you can't."

"Yes I can."

We went back and forth like that for a while.

By the end of the meeting, Andrea had earned a decal, a ribbon, a badge, a belt loop, a certificate, a medallion, and an extra marshmallow. Bummer in the summer!

But I got to eat my marshmallow first. So nah-nah-nah boo-boo on Andrea.

Beaver scouting was no fun. While we were waiting for Miss Blake to show up for our next meeting, we were all grumbling.

"I thought we were going to decorate pumpkins and make Popsicle-stick snow-man ornaments," said Alexia.

"I thought we were going to build race

cars out of wood," said Michael.

"I thought we were going to go spelunking," said Ryan.

"I'm thinking of quitting Beaver Scouts," I told the gang.

"Me too," everybody agreed.

We all stopped talking when Miss Blake arrived.

"I heard what you kids said about quitting," she barked. "Do you know what they call people who quit?"

"No, what?" we all asked.

"Quitters!" barked Miss Blake.

Well, that made sense.

"So you're not having fun, eh?" Miss Blake barked. "You want fun? Next week we're going on an overnight in the woods.

It will be more fun than you've ever had in your life."

"Yay!" we all shouted.

"But you never know what might happen out in the woods," barked Miss Blake. "You've got to be ready for *anything.* I hope you studied the part about first aid in the Beaver Scout Handbook."

"I did!" shouted the Human Homework Machine. "I also took a lifesaving class after school. When I get older, I'm going to get a job as a lifeguard."

Andrea takes classes in *everything* after school. If they gave a class in brushing your teeth, she would take that class so she could get better at it.

"Good job, Andrea!" barked Miss Blake.

"Life throws stuff at you when you least expect it. You've got to be prepared at all times. Let's say you're in the wilderness. Somebody faints and stops breathing. What do you do? It's an emergency!"

"You should break some glass," I said right away.

"Why would you do that?" asked Miss Blake.

"My family was at a hotel once," I replied. "There was a sign that said you should break glass in case of emergency."

Miss Blake slapped her own forehead.

"If somebody can't breathe, you should call 9-1-1," said Neil.

"You're in the wilderness!" barked Miss

Blake. "There's no time to call 9-1-1, and you probably don't have cell phone service anyway. The correct answer is that you should give that person mouth-to-mouth resuscitation."

Oh no, not *that.* I've seen mouth-to-mouth resuscitation. It looks a lot like kissing.

Miss Blake went to the closet and dragged out a big mannequin. It was the size of a grown-up man.

"This is Mr. Dummy," she barked. "He's not breathing."

"We've got to do something!" shouted Emily, as if Mr. Dummy was a real person.

"I'll show you what to do," barked Miss

Blake. She got down on her hands and knees, tilted Mr. Dummy's head back, pinched his nostrils shut, and started blowing air into his mouth.

Gross. I don't know about you, but I say kissing a dummy is weird. Kissing *anything* is weird. But kissing a dummy is *especially* weird.

"That looks hard," said Alexia. "I don't know if I could do that in an emergency."

"Hey, if you can't take the heat, get out of the kitchen," barked Miss Blake.

Huh? We weren't in a kitchen. What did kitchens have to do with anything?*

"I saved Mr. Dummy's life," barked Miss Blake. "He's breathing again."

"Yay!" everybody shouted, even though we all knew Mr. Dummy was never breathing in the first place.

"What do you do if somebody breaks an arm?" barked Miss Blake.

"Kiss the boo-boo and put a Band-Aid on it?" Emily guessed.

"No!" barked Miss Blake. "What do you

---

* If Mr. Dummy was in a kitchen instead of locked up in a closet, he probably wouldn't have fainted in the first place.

do if a tree falls on somebody's head and knocks them unconscious?"

"Punch the tree's face in?" I guessed.

"No! What do you do if somebody's bleeding out of their eyeballs? What do you do if somebody accidentally swallows a stapler? What do you do if somebody's leg falls off?"

"None of those things is going to happen," said Ryan.

"How do *you* know?" barked Miss Blake. "Stranger things have happened. Did I tell you about the time I was attacked by a bear?"

"Yes," we all replied. "You punched its face in."

"That's right!"

Miss Blake taught us what to do in case a coconut falls out of a tree and lands on your head. She taught us what to do in case anybody falls into a pit filled with poisonous snakes. She taught us what to do in case you get a squirrel stuck in your mouth. Andrea was taking notes the whole time.

"Okay, I think you kids are prepared for our overnight," barked Miss Blake. "I will see you in the school parking lot Saturday at one o'clock! Don't be late!"

Then we all got on the floor and did the Beaver Growl.

7 The Middle of Nowhere

It rained all week. I thought our overnight might be canceled. But on Friday my parents got a call saying it was on. They drove me to the parking lot, where all the kids were waiting on the bus.

"Can I come on the bus to take a few pictures?" my mom asked.

"No parents allowed!" Miss Blake barked. "Say good-bye!"

My mom said good-bye, and I climbed on the bus. I sat next to Ryan. We had already decided that we were going to share a tent together. Miss Blake stood up in the front of the bus as we pulled out of the parking lot.

"This is going to be fun," she barked. "Anybody who doesn't have fun will be punished."

We drove a million hundred miles to some forest. Finally, the bus pulled off to the side of the road, and we got out. There was a sign that warned about forest fires, poison ivy, flash floods, dehydration, and other scary stuff that can happen to you in the wilderness.

"Are we going to go spelunking?" asked Alexia.

"No! We hike!" barked Miss Blake as she grabbed a big backpack and a pair of binoculars.

"I love hiking and nature!" said Andrea.

Ugh. Hiking and nature are boring.

"Keep an eye out for bears or other wild animals," said Miss Blake.

"I'm scared," said Emily.

It would have been cool to see a bear or some other wild animal. But there weren't any animals. There were just lots of trees and rocks and birds. So Miss Blake talked about every tree, rock, and bird along the way. What a snoozefest.

"Look!" Miss Blake shouted, peering through her binoculars. "A red-billed nut-hatch!"

A bird is a bird, if you ask me. You've seen one bird, you've seen 'em all.

"I hope we see a snake," said Michael. "Snakes are cool."

"What would you do if you saw a snake?" Ryan asked.

"I'd punch its face in," I said.

After five minutes of hiking, I was bored. Nature is way overrated. We were in the middle of nowhere.*

* It would be cool if there was a town called Nowhere. Then you could go to the middle of it. Nobody ever goes to the edge of nowhere.

"This looks like the place where we started," said Neil.

"That's because we hiked a big loop," barked Miss Blake.

What? So we walked a million hundred miles in a *circle*? What was the point of that? If you're going to hike, you should hike someplace different.

"This looks like a good spot to set up

camp," said Miss Blake. "Let's pitch our tents here."

Why would you want to throw a tent? That made no sense at all.

"Where do you think Miss Blake got these tents?" Ryan asked.

"From Rent-A-Tent," I told him. "You can rent anything."

Ryan and I put up our tent together, while Miss Blake tied a string across two long sticks and stuck the sticks into the ground. Then she told us to gather up some wood.

"Are we going to build a fire?" asked Andrea.

"No, we're going to build *two* fires," said Miss Blake. She tied another string across two sticks and stuck them into the dirt next to the first ones. "One for the boys and one for the girls. Who can tell me what you need to start a fire?"

"Lighter fluid!" I shouted.

"No!" said Miss Blake. "Lighter fluid is for wimps."

"Fuel, air, and heat!" shouted Andrea,

who remembers everything she ever heard, saw, or read.

"That's right!" said Miss Blake. "You have air all around, of course. I'll give the boys' team and the girls' team three napkins. That's your fuel. You get one match to provide heat. Each team will build their fire under a rope. The first team to break their rope with the flame is the winner."

Yes! Boys against girls. Beating Andrea would be fun!

"I know how to build a fire," Andrea told Emily and Alexia. "We should carefully make a frame out of sticks and then light the napkins at the bottom."

"They're wasting their time," I whispered to the guys. "Just light the napkins and start piling sticks on top. Our fire will burn faster and we'll beat the girls."

Ryan lit the match. Michael held the napkins on the ground. Neil and I put thin sticks on top of the napkins. They started to catch fire.

"Burn! Burn! Burn!" we chanted as we piled more sticks on top. Our fire was getting bigger.

The girls finally finished building their dumb stack of sticks and lit it. The flames shot up so it was almost as high as ours.

Our fire got higher, and so did the girls' fire. In a few minutes, the flames were almost up to the two ropes. You couldn't tell which rope was going to break first.

You should have been there! There was electricity in the air.

Well, not exactly. It was just fire. If there was electricity in the air, we would have been electrocuted. But we were all on the edge of our seats.

Well, not really. There are no seats in the forest.

But it was exciting. Both flames were licking the ropes.

"Burn! Burn! Burn!" everybody chanted.

Smoke was coming off the ropes!

Both of the ropes were burning!

"Burn! Burn! Burn!"

And then . . . the girls' rope broke. *Nooooo!*

A second later, our rope broke.

"Yay!" shouted all the girls.

"Boo!" shouted all the boys.

8 The Universe Is Boring

I had to admit the girls won the campfire contest fair and square.

When both fires died down a little, Miss Blake got hot dogs from her backpack, and we cooked them. Yum! Then she got out a bag of marshmallows for us to toast. Double yum! I ate so many marshmallows, I thought I was gonna throw up. It was the greatest night of my life.

It was getting dark out. Miss Blake said she was going to rest in her tent, but we could spread our sleeping bags on the ground and talk for a while.

We were all lying on our backs looking at the sky. It was filled with stars. And it was weirdly quiet. There were no cars. No TVs. No noise.

"Isn't this peaceful?" asked Emily.

"Yeah," everybody replied.

"What do you see when you look up at the stars?" asked Andrea.

"I see stars," said Ryan.

"Maybe we'll see a shooting star," said Michael.

"Just think," said Andrea. "Those stars are *billions* of miles away. If the sun exploded, we wouldn't know it for eight minutes. That's how long it would take for the light to reach our eyes."

"I'm scared," said Emily.

"The universe is so big," said Alexia.

"Where do you think it ends?" asked Neil.

"Nobody knows," said Ryan.

"Maybe it *never* ends," said Michael.

"It can't go on forever," said Andrea. "It's got to end *somewhere*."

What a snoozefest. All this talk about the universe was boring.

"Hey, let's tell ghost stories," I suggested.

Ghost stories are cool, way cooler than talking about the universe.

"I'm scared," said Emily.

"Don't be scared," said Andrea. "Ghost stories are just stories. They're not real."

"I'll start!" I said, sitting up so everybody

could see me. I picked up my flashlight and held it under my chin, pointing up at my face.*

"Okay," I said. "Here's the story. There was this boy . . ."

"Yeah?" everybody said.

* Anytime you hold a flashlight under your chin in the dark, it looks like you're crazy. That's the first rule of being a kid.

"And he was out in the woods on an overnight," I said, lowering my voice to a whisper. "Like us."

"Yeah?"

"And it was pitch-dark. Just like now."

"Yeah?

"What happened next?" asked Andrea.

"A ghost came along and murdered him," I said. "The end."

"*That's* your story?" asked Andrea.

"It's a short story," I told her. "I cut out all the boring parts."

"Dude, that ghost story was lame," said Michael.

I said that if nobody liked my ghost story, they could tell a ghost story of their own. And somebody would have. But that's when the weirdest thing in the history of the world happened.

There was a noise behind us.

We turned around.

It was a bear!

I thought I was gonna die.

"Eeeeeeeekkkkkk!" we all screamed.

The bear was big and black and scary. I saw it with my own eyes!

Well, it would be pretty hard to see something with somebody else's eyes. But the bear was standing there about twenty feet away, staring at us.

"I'm s . . . s . . . scared!" said Emily, who had a reason to be scared for the first time in her life.

We were *all* scared. We didn't know what to say. We didn't know what to do. We had to think fast.

"Miss Blake!" shouted Andrea. "Come quick! It's an emergency!"

"M-m-m-maybe it's a friendly bear," Alexia whispered, "like Winnie-the-Pooh, or Paddington."

"Yeah," whispered Ryan. "Like Corduroy, or Fozzie Bear. They're friendly."

"Or the Three Bears," whispered Neil, "or the Care Bears or—"

"Grrrrrrrrrrrr!" growled the bear as it opened its mouth and showed its big teeth.

"Eeeeeeeekkkkkk!" we all screamed. I could smell the bear's bad breath.

"I d-d-don't think it's friendly," said Ryan.

Miss Blake came running out of her tent.

"What's going on out here?" she barked. "I was trying to get some–"

But she didn't have the chance to finish her sentence. Because that's when she noticed the bear.

"Grrrrrrrrrrrr!" growled the bear.

"Punch it in the face, Miss Blake!" shouted Ryan.

That's when the weirdest thing in the history of the world happened.

Miss Blake fainted! Her eyes rolled up in her head and she fell backward. Michael and Neil caught her just before she hit the ground.

"*Eeeeeeeekkkkkk!*" we all screamed.

"*Grrrrrrrrrrr!*" growled the bear.

"What are we going to do *now*?" shouted Neil.

"Emily!" Andrea shouted. "Quick! Climb up on my shoulders!"

"Why?" asked Emily. "I'm scared!"

"Just *do* it!" shouted Andrea. "If we make ourselves look big, it might scare the bear away!"

"How do you know that?" asked Michael.

"I read it in the Beaver Scout Handbook," Andrea replied.

We all helped Emily climb up onto Andrea's back.

"Now spread your arms out and make lots of noise!" Andrea shouted.

We all started yelling and screaming and hooting and hollering.

That's when the weirdest thing in the history of the world happened. The bear turned around and walked off into the woods.

"We did it!" Emily shouted excitedly. "He's leaving!"

Wow! Andrea should get the Nobel Prize. That's a prize they give out to people who don't have bells. I never knew you could scare a bear away just by pretending to be big and making noise.

I thought our overnight couldn't get more exciting than that. But then something even *more* exciting happened.

I'm not going to tell you what it was.

Okay, okay, I'll tell you. But you have to read the next chapter.*

---

* So nah-nah-nah boo-boo on you!

10
Saving Miss Blake

Everybody was happy that the bear ran away. But then we realized Miss Blake was still on the ground.

"She's not breathing!" shouted Alexia.

"We've got to *do* something!" shouted Emily.

"You have a smartphone, Andrea,"

shouted Michael. "Call 9-1-1!"

"There's no cell phone service out here!" Andrea shouted back.

"We should run and get help!" shouted Ryan.

"No time for that!" shouted Andrea. "Miss Blake could die! There's only one thing to do! We have to give her mouth-to-mouth resuscitation!"

Noooooooooo!

Ugh, gross. I wasn't going to do that. It's way too much like kissing.

"Move over!" Andrea barked.

She got down on her hands and knees and started blowing air into Miss Blake's mouth. Yuck.

"Is it working?" Ryan whispered while Andrea gave Miss Blake mouth-to-mouth resuscitation.

"I can't tell," whispered Neil.

"I guess Miss Blake isn't so brave after all," whispered Emily.

"And I'll bet she never punched a bear in the face," I said. "She's totally afraid of bears."

"I think she's waking up!" shouted Michael.

Miss Blake opened her eyes.

"Where am I?" she asked. "What happened to the bear?"

"It ran away," Andrea told her. "We're safe now."

"Thank goodness for that!" said Miss Blake.

As it turned out, we weren't safe at all. Because that's when the weirdest thing in the history of the world happened. There was a roaring sound in the distance.

"What's that?" asked Emily.

"It sounds like a jet engine!" I shouted.

But it wasn't a jet engine. It was the sound of rushing water.

It was a *wall* of water, and it was coming straight at us!

"WOW!" everybody said, which is "MOM" upside down.

"Run for your lives!" shouted Neil.

"It's a flash flood!" shouted Miss Blake.* "Try to grab on to something and hold on! Never leave your buddy behind!"

This was the worst thing to happen since TV Turnoff Week! Everybody was yelling and screaming and hooting and hollering and freaking out. We made a run for it.

But the wall of water caught up to us!

It knocked me over!

---

* Betcha didn't see *that* coming!

I started swimming!

I couldn't see anything!

My body was being thrown every which way!

Rocks were all around!

I bumped my head on something!

"Arlo, are you okay?" I heard Andrea shout.

And that was the last thing I remember.

The Big Surprise Ending

The next thing I knew, I was onstage in the all-porpoise room at school.* My head felt a little weird. I reached up to touch my forehead, and there was a bandage on it.

I looked around. The room was filled with our parents and teachers. All the

* That's a room that has no dolphins in it.

Beaver Scouts were onstage with me. So was Miss Blake.

"What's going on?" I whispered to Ryan, who was standing next to me.

"They're about to give out the award," he whispered back.

Our principal, Mr. Klutz, bounded up onto the stage. He held up his hand and made a peace sign, which means "Shut up."

"Welcome!" Mr. Klutz announced. "I hear you Beaver Scouts had quite an adventure this week. I'd like to introduce Miss Blake to tell us about it."

Miss Blake took the microphone. Everybody gave her a round of applause.

"These kids are tough, I'll tell you that," she said. "Toughest Beaver Scouts I've seen."

"What happened on your overnight?" asked Mr. Klutz.

"We took a nature hike," explained Miss Blake, "and we set up camp for the night. The kids made the fire, and we ate hot dogs and marshmallows. And the next thing we knew, we were attacked by a bear!"

"Gasp!" everybody gasped.

"What did you do?" asked Mr. Klutz.

"Well," said Miss Blake, "I was just about to punch that bear in the face when . . . the bear punched *me* in the face!"

"Gasp!" everybody gasped again.

What?! The bear never punched Miss Blake in the face! We knew the truth. She fainted when she saw the bear!

"The bear punched you in the face?" asked Mr. Klutz.

"Yes!" said Miss Blake. "Isn't that right, kids?"

I looked at Ryan. Ryan looked at Michael. Michael looked at Neil. Neil looked at Emily. Emily looked at Andrea. We were all looking at each other.

"Yes, Miss Blake," Andrea said. "The bear punched you in the face."

"I was knocked unconscious," Miss Blake continued. "What happened next–well, I'd better let these brave Beaver Scouts tell you."

"We were all scared," Andrea said. "Emily climbed up on my back and we made loud noises to scare the bear away."

"And then Andrea gave Miss Blake mouth-to-mouth resuscitation until she woke up," added Emily.

Andrea smiled the smile that she smiles to let everybody know how wonderful she is.

"Wow, that's some story!" said Mr. Klutz.

"That's not the end of it," said Miss Blake. "What happened after that, kids?"

"There was a flash flood!" said Michael.

"It came out of nowhere!" said Ryan. "Water was everywhere!"

"We thought we were gonna die!" I said.

"Gasp!" everybody gasped.

"What happened after that?" asked Mr. Klutz.

"All our supplies got swept away by the water!" said Andrea.

"And then *we* got swept away by the water!" said Emily.

"Arms and legs were everywhere!" said Ryan.

I didn't know what happened after that.

"After that," Neil said, "A.J. bumped his head on a rock."

"Andrea saved his life!" said Emily.

What? I didn't know about *that* part.

"A.J. was drowning!" said Alexia.

"Andrea swam over and dragged him out of the water!" said Emily.

What?!

"She gave him mouth-to-mouth resuscitation until he started breathing again," said Alexia.

"Wait. WHAT?!" I shouted.

"Andrea gave you mouth-to-mouth resuscitation," said Alexia. "She saved your life!"

"Noooooooooooooo!" I shouted, wiping off my mouth. "Disgusting!"

"It's true, A.J.!" said Neil. "It looked like she was kissing you."

"Oooooh, Andrea and A.J. were kissing," said Ryan. "They must be in *love*!"

"When are you gonna get married?" asked Michael.

It was the worst moment of my life. I wanted to run away to Antarctica and go live with the penguins. Penguins don't have to give each other mouth-to-mouth resuscitation.

"Well, that's gratitude for you!" complained Andrea. "Arlo, I'm never going to save your life *again*!"

That's pretty much what happened. Miss Blake said she was really proud of us. She gave each of us a sticker, a decal, a ribbon, a badge, a belt loop, a certificate, a medallion, and a plaque that said how brave we were. Then she gave Andrea the Busy Beaver of the Year Award. Her parents took pictures.

Maybe Miss Blake will admit she's afraid of bears. Maybe people will stop taking pictures of cheese. Maybe we'll go spelunking. Maybe Andrea will take a class in brushing your teeth. Maybe Mr. Dummy will stop breathing again. Maybe beavers will start chatting about what they're going to have for dinner. Maybe I'll let the guys talk me into signing up to be a Beaver Scout again next year.

But it won't be easy!